3 4028 09495 6118
HARRIS COUNTY PUBLIC LIBRARY

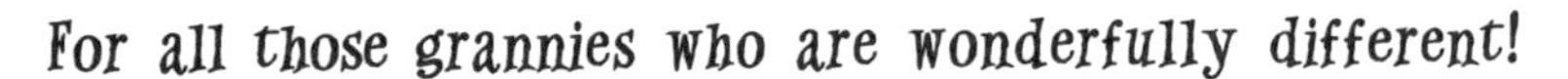

For all those grannies who are wonderfully different!

T. C.

For Granny Sue, who wears funny hats, and Granny Clare,

who cooks a mean froggy-poop soup

J. B.

First U.S. edition 2012

Library of Congress Cataloging-in-Publication Data is available.
Library of Congress Catalog Card Number pending
ISBN 978-0-7636-5904-2

12 13 14 15 16 17 JIA 10 9 8 7 6 5 4 3 2 1

Printed in Guanlan, Shenzhen, China

This book was typeset in Witches Magic.
The illustrations were done in pen, brush-pen, and digital.

Nosy Crow an imprint of
Candlewick Press
99 Dover Street
Somerville, Massachusetts 02144

www.nosycrow.com
www.candlewick.com

HUBBLE BUBBLE, GRANNY TROUBLE

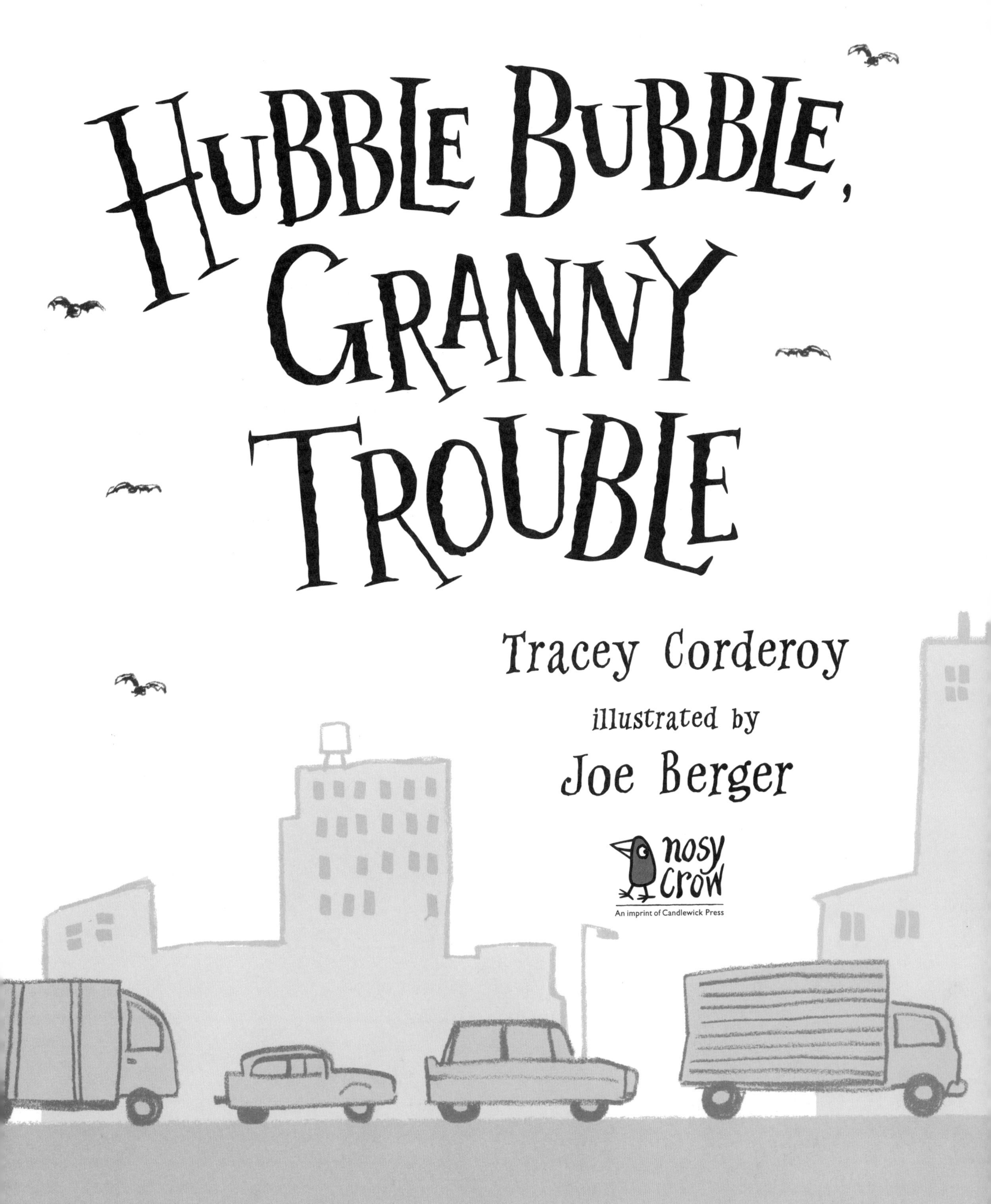

Tracey Corderoy

illustrated by

Joe Berger

nosy crow

An imprint of Candlewick Press

My granny's kind of different.

She wears black pointy hats.
And everywhere she goes she takes
her cats and frogs and bats—
even to the movies,
which she thinks is fine.
Especially as Granny never
has to wait in line!

SLUDGE
SPRINKLES
WHAT A
WIZARD
IDEA!!

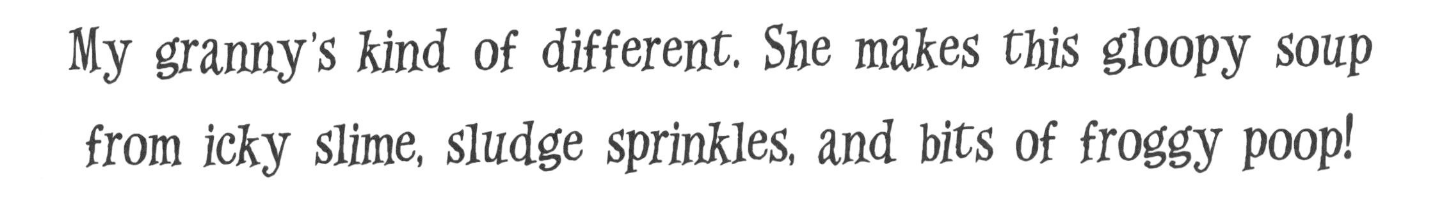

My granny's kind of different. She makes this gloopy soup from icky slime, sludge sprinkles, and bits of froggy poop!

I ask for chicken fingers, but Granny shakes her head.

"Oh, yuck!" she cries. "How horrible! Here—have some soup instead!"

My granny's kind of different. Her friends are different, too.

Why can't they do the sort of things

that **other** grannies do?

They like to make things disappear. My friends all think it's cool.

But one day things just went too far
when Granny helped at school!

c-a-t spells...
octo-
pota-
noceros

My granny's kind of different. She drives a crazy car
that's got no roof or seats or wheels—
it's really just bizarre!

While others sit in traffic, she makes that car-thing fly.

"Hey, Granny, please slow down!"

I shout as we go zooming by.

My granny's kind of different. So one day, "Gran," I said, "how about we try to make you normal-ish instead?"

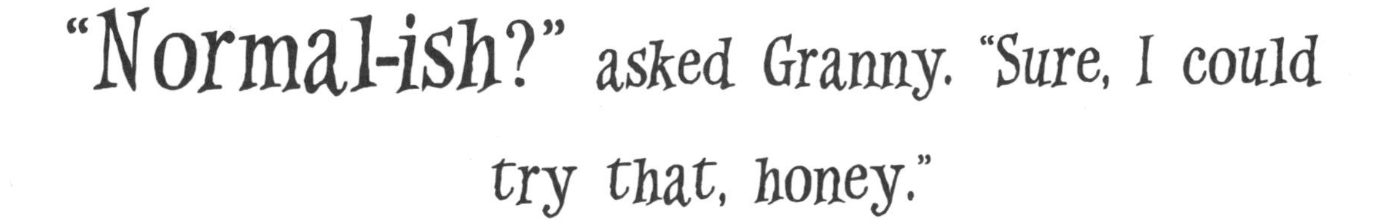

"Normal-ish?" asked Granny. "Sure, I could try that, honey."

And so we sat and knitted hats . . . though Gran's was

kind of

funny.

Later on, we caught the bus
and rode it into town.
"See?" I said. "No zooming!
No flying
upside down!"

We went inside the pet shop
to choose a normal pet.
No fangs, no warts, not green or black—
as cute as you could get!

Then Granny got her hair done, all normal-ish and neat—
combed and curled and nicely twirled—
I thought she looked quite sweet!

Though Gran looked nice and normal now, something wasn't right.
She seemed like someone else's gran
as we strolled home that night.

I went to see her the next day,
but she was still in bed.

"Oh, Gran!" I cried.
"What's wrong with you?"
"I'm kind of . . . **bored**!" she said.

We went down to the kitchen
and I made some gloopy soup.
(I stirred in lots of slime and added extra froggy poop!)

I looked across the table. "I'm sorry, Gran," I said.
"You were fun and different,
but now you're sad instead."

"Not for long!" cried Granny, shaking out her bun.
"All my friends are due at two to have some granny fun!"

So Granny got things ready
while I let in the bats,
searched the flowerpots for frogs,
and called in all the cats.

My granny's kind of different. That's how she's meant to be.

I love my granny as she is and know that

she loves me!

We're going on a little trip,
but won't need knitted hats—

just bathing suits . . .

some cats and frogs

and lots and lots of bats!
BURP!